a cat,

a rat

and a duck.

3

Once, there was a little red hen. She lived on a farm in a little white hut.

She was always
looking for food.

Her three best friends lived on the farm too.

Meow!

There was a proud black cat.

There was a fat rat.

And there was a very
noisy duck.

One day, the little red hen saw some grains of wheat. She looked at them.

If I plant these, they will grow.

She looked at her friends.

"I'm busy," purred the cat.

"So am I," squeaked
the rat.

"Me too!" the duck
quacked.

"Then I shall plant them myself," said the little red hen.

She found a sunny field and buried the grains of wheat in the ground.

Every day she
watered them.

A few shoots began
to show.

Slowly, they grew...

...into a patch
of golden wheat.

"Who will help me cut down the wheat?" asked the little red hen.

"I'm busy," purred the cat.

"So am I," squeaked the rat.

"Me too!" the duck quacked.

"Then I shall cut it down myself," said the little red hen.

And she did.

"I need to carry the wheat to the mill. I want to grind it into flour," she said.

There was a lot of wheat.

"Who will help me carry it?" she asked.

22

"Then I shall carry the wheat myself," said the little red hen.

She scooped the wheat
into a basket.

It was heavy, but she
carried it all by herself.

"Who will help me grind the wheat into flour?" she asked.

"I'm busy," purred the cat.

"So am I," squeaked
the rat.

"Me too!" the
duck quacked.

"Then I will grind it myself," said the little red hen.

"Who will help me bake the flour into bread?" she asked.

By now, she could guess
the answer.

"I'm busy," purred the cat.

"So am I," squeaked
the rat.

"Me too!" the duck
quacked.

"Well then, I shall bake it myself," said the little red hen.

She took the flour to
the bakehouse...

...and put on
her apron
and hat.

She put the flour in a bowl,
with water, oil, salt
and yeast...

...and stirred them to
make a soft mixture.

She pushed, folded and
turned it around...

...and left it in
a warm place.

In two hours, it was twice as big! She put it in a hot oven to bake.

Soon the most delicious
smell floated out into
the farmyard.

Mmmm...

"That smells good,"
purred the cat.

The rat got up from under his tree. His nose twitched.

The duck got out of the pond. He waddled over to the bakehouse too.

The little red hen took the
bread out of the oven.

What a
perfect loaf!

"Who will help me eat the bread?" she asked.

"I will!" purred the cat.

"And me!" squeaked
the rat.

"Me too!" the
duck quacked.

"Oh no you won't," said the little red hen. "I shall eat it all myself."

And she did!

About the story

The Little Red Hen is an old, old folk tale. It has been around for hundreds of years. No one knows who first told it, but it probably came from Russia.

Designed by Laura Nelson Norris
Series designer: Russell Punter
Series editor: Lesley Sims

First published in 2019 by Usborne Publishing Ltd.,
Usborne House, 83-85 Saffron Hill, London EC1N 8RT, England.
www.usborne.com Copyright © 2019 Usborne Publishing Ltd.